Freddie Gets Dressed

Nicola Smee

• little • barron's •

My bear's bare
and so am I.
I think we'd better
get dressed.

this
·little·barron's·
book belongs to

....

....

Underpants for me
and
underpants for Bear.

T-shirt for me
and
T-shirt for Bear.

Socks for me
and
socks for Bear.

Shorts for
me and …
I think a skirt for
Bear today.

Shoes for me
and
shoes for Bear.

Oh, no!
It's back to being
bare, Bear!